THREE HORSES

Movie Madness

A 4D BOOK

by Cari Meister

illustrated by Heather Burns

PICTURE WINDOW BOOKS
a capstone imprint

Three Horses is published by Picture Window Books,
A Capstone Imprint
1710 Roe Crest Drive
North Mankato, Minnesota 56003
www.mycapstone.com

Text © 2019 Picture Window Books
Illustrations © 2019 Picture Window Books

Library of Congress Cataloging-in-Publication Data is available
on the Library of Congress website.
ISBN: 978-1-5158-2950-8 (library binding)
ISBN: 978-1-5158-2954-6 (paperback)
ISBN: 978-1-5158-2958-4 (eBook PDF)

Designer:
Lori Bye

Printed and boudn in the USA
PA017

Download the Capstone app!

- Ask an adult to download the Capstone 4D app.
- Scan the cover and stars inside the book for additional content.

When you scan a spread, you'll find
fun extra stuff to go with this book!
You can also find these things
on the web at www.capstone4D.com
using the password: threehorses.29508

TABLE OF CONTENTS

CHAPTER 1

A Party Plan

It was dinnertime at Farley Farms. Toni, the barn manager, slipped some hay into Princess' stall.

Princess stamped her hoof and put her nose up in disgust. "Really?" she said. "Hay again? When is Toni going to take off her blinders? I am a cat. Not a horse."

Seb, the draft horse in the next stall, smiled to himself. He looked at Princess. Her mane was braided. Her owner, Melody, had laced a fuchsia bow into her tail. She had sparkly hoof polish on her hooves

"I'm afraid Toni may always think you are a horse," said Seb.

"Oh poo!" said Princess. "That's what I was afraid of!"

Princess sulked in the corner. She liked Farley Farms enough. Toni was a nice barn manager. She had two good horse friends. Seb and The Blizzard, an older fat little Shetland pony. Most people called The Blizzard by his barn name, Snowy. But Princess knew he preferred to be called The Blizzard, so she tried to respect that.

Princess let out a deep sigh. *If only I could get out every night, like a real cat. Then I would be really happy,* she thought.

"Cheer up," said Seb. "Did you know it's Snowy's birthday today?"

Princess' eyes opened wide. "We MUST have a party!" she said.

"A party would be fun," said Seb. "But what about a *Tres Caballos Incognito* birthday adventure?"

Tres Caballos Incognito means "Three horses in disguise." It was the name Snowy gave the trio when they escaped the barn, wearing their fly masks.

"Oh yes!" said Princess.

"How about going to the zoo?" asked Seb.

"What's the point in that?" said Princess. "To stare at other animals? Boring! How about going to the ice cream parlor? Cats LOVE ice cream. We could get a giant sundae and lick it all up."

"I think Snowy is lactose intolerant," said Seb. "Remember that time his owner gave him some yogurt? He groaned for three days."

Princess frowned. "What should we do then?" she asked.

Seb and Princess looked out through their stall bars.

Toni was walking down the aisle, talking on her phone. "I heard that movie called *Yul the Reindeer* was really good. Where is it showing? What time? 7:00? Perfect. See you then," she said.

Seb and Princess looked at each other. The movies! Why didn't they think of that?

"The movies are *purrfect*!" said Princess. "The Blizzard's always talked about going to see a movie."

CHAPTER 2

An Alarm Goes Off

By the time Toni had turned off the lights for the night, Princess and Seb had come up with a plan.

"But how are we going to get in the theater without being discovered?" asked Princess.

"And how are we going to get popcorn?" asked Seb. "I've always wanted to try popcorn."

Princess shrugged. "I guess we will just figure it out when we get there. Now use your skills and get us out of here."

"OK," said Seb. He put his lips around the latch and pulled. Soon he was standing in the aisle. A minute later, Princess was standing next to him.

They trotted down the aisle to Snowy's stall. He was asleep.

"Ahem!" said Seb. He tapped his front hoof. "OK, one, two, three."

"Happy Birthday to you! Happy Birthday to you! Happy Birthday dear THE BLIZZARD, Happy Birthday to you," they sang.

Snowy stretched and shook his mane.

"You remembered!" he said. "I thought you forgot!"

"Of course not!" said Seb.

"We have a surprise birthday plan," sang Princess.

Seb wrapped his lips around Snowy's latch and slid open the furry pony's door.

Snowy trotted out.

"We need our masks," said Princess. "That way, if someone sees us, they won't know who we are."

"Great idea," said Snowy. He trotted up to the front door and grabbed a bag from his hiding spot. He pulled out three fly masks.

"Where are we going?" he asked as they put on the masks.

"It's a surprise," said Princess.

"OK," said Snowy. "Do you know how to get there?"

Seb and Princess looked at each other and blinked.

"That's what I thought," said Snowy. "Let me look it up." Snowy pulled his laptop from the bag. He turned it on. Then he grabbed a hoof pick with his mouth and started pecking at the keys.

This didn't surprise Seb and Princess.

They were used to Snowy typing away. After all, he was writing a novel, *From the Horse's Mouth*.

"So where are we going?" he asked, as Seb opened the big barn door. But as he opened the door, an alarm sounded.

Tres Caballos Incognito bolted down the driveway.

The sound got quieter the farther they galloped down the road.

"What was that?" asked Seb.

"I have no idea!" said Princess.

From the other direction, they heard another siren—WEE, OHH, WEE, OHH. A cop car was buzzing down the road toward Farley Farms.

AAWWWW! The horses stood in the middle of road, snorting. They looked in all directions.

"Let's hide in the trees," said Princess.

"Good idea," said Snowy. "The noises can't get us there."

CHAPTER 3

Princess Disappears

Tres Caballos Incognito hid in the trees. Soon the noises stopped.

"What a crazy night!" said Seb.

"I wonder what is going on," said Snowy.

Seb shrugged.

"So where are we going?" asked Snowy.

Seb opened his mouth into a big, toothy grin. "The movies!" he said.

"The movies?" said Snowy. "How wonderful! I've always wanted to go to the movies. What are we going to see?"

"*Yul the Reindeer,*" said Seb.

Snowy pulled out his laptop and typed:
YUL THE REINDEER.

He read, "*Yul the Reindeer* is sure to delight even the most finicky movie critic. It has it all—adventure, beautiful scenery, cute animals, and romance." Snowy looked up.

"It sounds great!" said Princess. "It has all the elements I love in books."

Seb looked confused. "What does *finicky* mean?"

Snowy typed it into his computer. He cleared his throat. "*The Horse's Dictionary* writes: *finicky means picky, persnickety, fussy, or critical.*"

Seb rolled his eyes. "I totally get it," he said.

"Princess, does that make sense to you?" asked Snowy.

But Princess wasn't there.

"Princess! Where are you?" called Snowy.

Princess didn't answer.

Seb was annoyed. "How could she just take off like that?" he asked. "We might be late for the movie!"

Snowy whinnied into the dark. "Princess!"

Princess did not whinny back.

CHAPTER 4

A Rabbit

Princess was busy chasing a rabbit across the field.

Finally, she thought. *Some real feline action.*

The rabbit was fast.

But Princess was fast too. She gritted her teeth and ran like the wind.

The rabbit stopped for a second to look back. He wondered what on earth a horse was doing chasing him. Surely, she was not going to eat him. So he stopped.

Princess stopped too.

is he stopping? she wondered. *This
. . . ust getting fun! Doesn't he know that
the fun is in the chase? Now I have to just
. at him.*

Princess bent her long head down
next to the rabbit. She sniffed. Then . . .
AAAACHOOO! She sneezed.

She sniffed again.

AAAACHOO!

Her sneeze was so loud that Seb and Snowy heard her.

They came galloping over.

"What are you doing over here?" asked Seb. "We are going to be late for the movie!"

But Princess was slumped over. She was crying.

"I can't believe it!" she said. "I finally caught a rabbit."

"Well, that's good news, right?" asked Snowy.

"Yes. But I can't eat it," cried Princess.

"Well," said Seb, "horses are not supposed—"

"What happened?" asked Snowy, nudging Seb for his slip-up.

"Didn't you hear me sneeze?" said rincess. "I must be allergic to rabbits!"

Seb wanted to feel sorry for her, but he couldn't. He wanted to get to the movie. "I bet you aren't allergic to popcorn," he said. "Let's get going!"

Snowy patted Princess on the shoulder. "It's always hard to find out what we don't want to know. But try to look on the bright side. We are going to the movies!"

CHAPTER 5

A Box

By the time Snowy figured out the best route to the theater, Princess got over her sadness.

"Oooh! I can't wait," she said. They trotted through the back alleys to get to the theater.

"Let's hide behind that dumpster," said Snowy. "We don't want to be seen."

"How are we going to get into the theater?" asked Princess. "It's not like we can walk in the front door."

"Wait here," said Snowy. "I will scop out. Don't worry. I will stick to the shado.

Seb grabbed a large box from the dumpster. "Put this on," he said.

"How will I see?" asked Snowy.

"Give me your hoof pick," said Seb.

Snowy handed Seb the pick.

"There," said Seb as he poked three holes in the box.

Seb placed the box over Snowy.

"How do I look?" Snowy asked.

"You look like a box," said Princess.

"Well, I guess it's working then," said Snowy.

Snowy slowly walked toward the back door of the theater. Just as he got within two strides, the door creaked opened.

CHAPTER 6

Statues

A man from the theater stared at the big box in front of him. Snowy froze.

The man scratched his head. "That's strange. I thought I put that box in the dumpster," he said. The man was carrying a big trash bag. He tapped the top of the box. "I'll be back for you," he said to the box.

It was a loud, scary sound. Snowy did everything he could to stop from getting scared. If he got scared, he would poop. The man would find the horses, and the birthday adventure would be over.

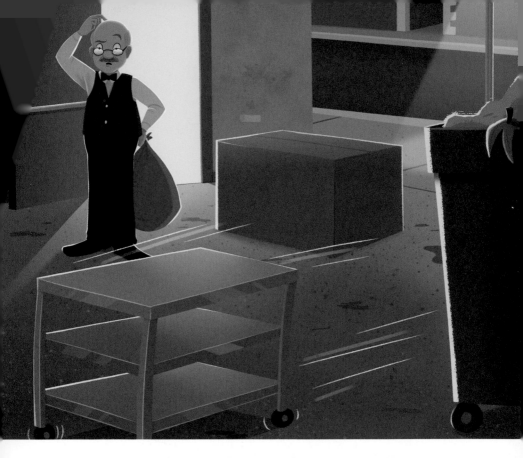

The man left the box and started walking
toward the dumpster.

"Oh no!" said Snowy.

But Princess and Seb were one step ahead.

Seb found a rolling cart behind the
dumpster. He pushed it in the opposite
direction. It rolled and crashed in the far alley.

"What is going on around here?" said movie man. As he walked over to the alley, *Tres Caballos Incognito* scrambled around the corner. They snuck through the back door of the theater.

Seb closed the door. "You can only open it from the inside," he said, smiling. "That man will have to go to the front to get back in. That will give us more time to find where to go."

"Good thinking," said Snowy.

The three friends poked their heads into the lobby. The movie was about to start, so there were few people around.

Seb stuck his nose in the air and inhaled. "I smell popcorn!" he said.

Just then, a small boy turned around. His eyes got big. He tugged on his mother's sleeve. "Mommy! Mommy!" he said. "This theater has real horses!"

Seb, Snowy, and Princess froze.

The mother was too busy chatting with another lady to turn around. "That's nice dear," she said without looking.

"Mommy, Mommy!" said the boy. "Look!"

"Stay very, very still," said Snowy. "Pretend you are a statue."

The boy's mother finally turned around. She squinted. "Those are just cardboard horses," she said. "They make them look so real."

The boy didn't believe her. His mother took him by the hand and led him into the theater.

"Phew!" said Seb.

"That was close!" said Princess.

"The movie is almost starting," said Snowy. "I bet we can sneak in now."

Somehow they did.

CHAPTER 7

Yul the Reindeer

It was Tuesday. There were only a handful of people in the theater. *Tres Caballos Incognito* found a wide row of seats in the back. The movie was just starting. No one seemed to notice them.

"We didn't get any popcorn!" said Seb.

"Maybe after the movie is over, we will find a half-eaten bag," said Snowy.

Seb hoped that would be true.

The music got louder as Yul the reindeer made his first appearance on the big screen. He was majestic!

"Wow," whispered Princess. "If I was a hooved mammal, I might love him."

The three friends watched as Yul met a beautiful reindeer named Holly. They were perfect together. But one day, Holly got lost in a blizzard.

"Go find her," Seb whispered to Yul on the screen. "You must find your true love!"

Yul seemed to listen. He crunched through the blizzard searching for Holly. Soon he came to a big lake.

"The ice is too thin," whispered Snowy. "Go back through the woods instead."

Unfortunately, Yul did not listen to Snowy's advice.

Yul slowly stepped onto the thin ice. The music rose.

"I can't watch!" said Princess. She buried her head under her leg, but peeked through just enough so she could still see.

The ice began to *crack, crack, crack* . . . and then it broke. Yul splashed into the icy waters. He scrambled to get back up on the ice, but he couldn't get a grip. It was too slippery. Then all of a sudden there was a ROAR!

Yul turned around. It was a grizzly bear!

The audience screamed. Princess hid her face. And Seb? He just couldn't help it. He was so scared, he dropped a large pile of steaming poo.

Snowy noticed right away.

"Seb!" said Snowy.

"I'm so sorry!" Seb said. "I couldn't help it!"

The audience noticed too.

"What is that smell?" someone yelled in the dark.

The movie man came in with a flashlight.

Tres Caballos Incognito tried to hide. But there was nowhere to go.

The flashlight beam revealed the horses in all their glory.

The movie man jumped back.

"Stop the movie," he shouted. "Turn on the lights!"

"Nothing to do now, but just own it," said Snowy. "Look like the noble steeds we are. Perhaps they won't get too mad."

"No chance I'm going to get any popcorn now," Seb said.

The big lights clicked on.

CHAPTER 8

New Friends

The moviegoers gasped. One big man up front laughed.

The boy smiled. "See mommy!" he said. "I told you there were horses in here."

Just then, a familiar voice appeared. "What on earth?"

It was Toni. She was at the movie too. She walked up to the horses. "Snowy? Princess? Seb?" she asked.

The movie man glared at her. "Do you know these horses?" he asked. "Did you bring them here? What were you thinking?"

Toni stumbled a bit. "Yes, I know them. No, I didn't bring them here. I am not sure how they escaped. I just put in a new alarm system. If they got out, I should have been notified."

Princess rubbed her head against Toni. She was glad Toni was here.

Toni pulled her phone from her pocket. The screen was black.

"I forgot that I turned my phone off for the movie," she said.

Toni turned her phone back on. There were five alerts flashing.

"I am so sorry," said Toni. "I will get them out of here right away." She picked up her purse and popcorn.

Seb saw his chance. He nudged his way closer and grabbed the bag.

The audience laughed.

"I guess he wants some popcorn," said the big man up front.

The little boy ran up. "Are they friendly?" he asked.

"Yes," said Toni.

The moviegoers came closer. "Look at the little white one. He is so cute! Can we pet him?"

Toni nodded. "Sure," she said. "He likes the attention."

It was true. Snowy loved it.

The moviegoers oohed and ahhed. They asked Toni questions as they petted and fed the horses popcorn.

"And that big one—is he a draft horse of some kind?"

"Do you think they liked the movie?"

"Are reindeer related to horses?" asked another.

Next, they all wanted selfies with the horses. Then they wanted to watch the movie. They convinced the movie man to start it again.

"Well, OK," he said, looking at Toni. "But can you clean that up first?" The man nodded toward Seb's pile.

"Of course," said Toni. "I will just run out to my truck and grab a shovel from the back."

CHAPTER 9

Happily Ever After

By the time the three friends were back in their stalls, they were tired but happy.

"That was the best birthday ever," said Snowy. "Thank you."

"It was a great movie," said Seb. "I can't believe Yul was able to fight off the bear."

"Yes, but not before losing a leg!" said Princess. "I can't believe he hopped all that way to rescue Holly."

"Then they lived happily ever after," said Snowy.

"Yes," said Princess. "Happily ever after."

Snowy pulled out his computer. He typed for a little bit.

"What are you writing?" asked Seb.

"I just finished adding a famous quote to my novel. I was reminded of it tonight at the theater. It is from the ancient Greek philosopher Xenophon."

"What did he say?" yawned Princess.

Snowy cleared his throat. He read:

"And indeed, a horse who bears himself proudly is a thing of such beauty and astonishment that he attracts the eyes of all beholders.

No one will tire of looking at him as long as he will display himself in all his splendor."

"People love us don't they?" asked Seb.

"Yes, they do," said Snowy. "But they should. We are noble creatures. There is not another animal as glorious as the horse."

"I'm glad you are my friend," said Seb. "You help me see things."

"I'm glad you are my friend too," said Snowy. "Besides, we'd never get out of here for adventures if it was not for you. Isn't that true, Princess?"

But Princess was already asleep, dreaming of an adventure yet to come.

GLOSSARY

advice—suggestions about what to do about a problem

allergic—when something, like a bee sting or pollen in the air, makes someone feel sick; many allergies make you sneeze

critic—a person who points out the good and bad in something

disguise—clothing that hides you by making you look like something else

disgust—a strong feeling of dislike

feline—any animal of the cat family

fly mask—a mask used to protect a horse's eyes and jaw from flies

glorious—wonderful, beautiful

lactose intolerant—when someone's body is not able to process a certain type of sugar found in milk and dairy products

mammal—a warm-blooded animal that breathes air; mammals have hair or fur

noble—something or someone that looks to be of high rank or upper class

philosopher—a person who studies truth and knowledge

respect—to believe in the quality and worth of others and yourself

route—the road or course followed to get somewhere

steed—a horse, especially one that is lively

sulk—to act angry and silent

ABOUT THE AUTHOR

Cari Meister has written more than 130 books for children, including the Tiny series (Penguin) and the Fast Forward Fairy Tales series (Scholastic). Cari is a school librarian and she loves to visit other schools and libraries to talk about the joy of reading and writing. Cari lives in the mountains of Colorado with her husband, four boys, one horse, and one dog.

ABOUT THE ILLUSTRATOR

Heather Burns is an illustrator from a small town called Uttoxeter in the UK. In 2013, she graduated from the University of Lincoln with a degree in illustration and has been working as a freelance illustrator ever since. Heather has a passion for bringing stories to life with pictures and hopes that her work makes people smile. When she's not working she's usually out walking her grumpy black Labrador, Meadow!

TALK ABOUT IT

1. Are *Tres Caballos Incognito* good friends? Give three examples from the story to support your answer.

2. Seb and Snowy never try to convince Princess that she's a horse. Why do you think that is?

3. Was the audience's reaction to *Tres Caballos Icognito* surprising to you? Why or why not?

WRITE ABOUT IT

1. Write a different ending! What would've happened if Toni hadn't been in the theater?

2. Write a chapter of Snowy's *From the Horse's Mouth*.

3. Write the last chapter from the movie worker's point of view. What does he think about the horses in the theater?

BOOKS IN THE
THREE HORSES SERIES

THE FUN
DOESN'T STOP HERE!

Discover more at
www.capstonekids.com

Videos & Contests
Games & Puzzles
Friends & Favorites
Authors & Illustrators